The
Tale
of
Peter Rabbit

FREDERICK WARNE

Published by the Penguin Group
Penguin Books Ltd, 27 Wrights Lane, London W8 5TZ, England
Penguin Putnam Inc., 375 Hudson Street, New York, N.Y. 10014, USA
Penguin Books Canada Ltd, 10 Alcorn Avenue, Toronto, Ontario, Canada M4V 3B2
Penguin Books (NZ) Ltd, Private Bag 102902, NSMC, Auckland, New Zealand
Penguin Books India (P) Ltd, 11 Community Centre, Panchsheel Park, New Delhi 110 017, India
Penguin Books (South Africa) (Pty) Ltd, 5 Watkins Street, Denver Ext 4, 2094, South Africa

Penguin Books Ltd, Registered Offices: Harmondsworth, Middlesex, England

Visit our web site at: www.peterrabbit.com

This edition first published by Frederick Warne 2001

1 3 5 7 9 10 8 6 4 2

ISBN: 07232 4717 X

Additional illustrations by Colin Twinn and Alex Vining

Colour reproduction by Saxon Photolitho
Printed and bound in Singapore by Tien Wah Press

The Tale of Peter Rabbit

Based on the original tale
BY BEATRIX POTTER

FREDERICK WARNE

This is Peter Rabbit.

He lives here with his
mother, Mrs Rabbit, and
his sisters, Flopsy, Mopsy
and Cotton-tail.

One morning
Mrs Rabbit said,
"I am going out,
children. Now run
along, but don't go into
Mr McGregor's garden."

Then Mrs Rabbit took
her basket and her
umbrella and walked
through the wood.

Flopsy, Mopsy and Cotton-tail were good little rabbits. They went to pick blackberries.

But Peter was a naughty little rabbit. He ran to Mr McGregor's garden and squeezed under the gate!

Peter sat in the garden
and ate lots of radishes.

Then, feeling rather sick,
he went to look for some
parsley to make him
feel better.

But round the corner
he met ...

. . . Mr McGregor!

Mr McGregor ran after
Peter Rabbit, waving
a rake and shouting,
"Stop thief!"

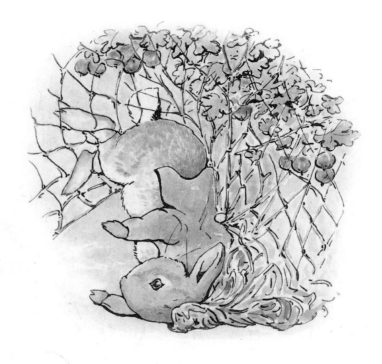

Peter ran into a net
and got caught by the
buttons on his blue jacket.

Then Mr McGregor
tried to trap Peter with
a sieve!

Peter wriggled out but he
lost his jacket and shoes.

Peter jumped into a
watering-can.

Mr McGregor was
looking for him
underneath the flowerpots.

Then Peter jumped out
of a window and
knocked over some
flowerpots. He got away!

Mr McGregor was tired
of running after Peter.

He went back to his work.

Peter heard the *scritch, scratch* of Mr McGregor's hoe. He climbed on to a wheelbarrow and looked across the garden.

He could see the gate!

Peter ran as fast as he could go. Mr McGregor saw him but Peter didn't care. He slipped under the gate and was safe at last.

When Peter got home,
he was so tired that he
flopped down on to
the floor.

Mrs Rabbit was
cooking. "Where have
you been, Peter Rabbit?"
she said.

Peter Rabbit was not very well. Mrs Rabbit put him to bed and made him some tea.

But Flopsy, Mopsy and
Cotton-tail had bread
and milk and blackberries
for supper.